STEPS

by MONA SIMPSON

I didn't believe in forgiveness, particularly.

This all began when I decided to de-clutter my in-box. *De-clutter* is a compound word that makes Harry say "middle age." He jokes about having a lover who wears a dental splint. He's teasing, but he probably minds my age. I would.

I do. But I'm an actress. If I didn't mind, I'd be a moron.

I was deleting, deleting, deleting when I came to yet another message from an unknown sender. Dirk Vanderhoff turned out to be my agent's secretary's secretary. Apparently, my agent's *secretary*, the young woman who always remained on the line when Solange called, had been fielding messages, and after three from the same person, she told Dirk to hear out the caller's story. She sounded like a decent person, Dirk Vanderhoff wrote, so they didn't know if I'd want them to pass my numbers along? The caller had told this assistant's assistant that her boyfriend was the son of my once-upon-a-time stepfather, Bruce Justin.

"Sure," I must have zinged, then, delete!

My mother had left Bruce Justin when I was fourteen. We drove out of town in the middle of the night and she divorced him from another state a year later. I hadn't seen or spoken to him since. Once, after a decade, some friend of my mother's had sent her a Christmas card showing Bruce with his second wife and four sons in matching red turtlenecks. Each wore a hat that supported reindeer antlers made of felt. Bruce's rack was larger than the others. My mother's friend had written "*In*teresting" with three exclamation marks.

The caller—who was attached to one of those antlered boys, grown-up—had told Dirk Vanderhoff that she was trying to reach me because Bruce, our only possible point of intersection in this vast ballroom of three hundred million, was dying. Apparently, due to that, I needed to talk to a complete stranger.

It was the son who phoned me. My first thought was: *How* did you get my number again? This was what my minor fame had gotten me. Not enough money, not much fun, not even a plausible date (Harry, preposterously young, was my ex-trainer—though he'd graduated from far better schools than I had, that's Hollywood—and I constantly reminded him, *This can't last*), but an extra duty: the late-life problems of a person who otherwise couldn't have found me, and who may not even have wanted to. I wondered if Bruce Justin needed money.

"He was real proud of you with your movies," the son said. "He kept the DVDs by his desk. Showed them to people. Always said he was your stepfather."

Stepfather? I thought. Really? Doesn't the term expire? It had been thirty-five years since my mother took her children and the silver and left in a car she'd already packed with what little else we had that was precious.

"He's got cancer of the throat," Bruce Justin's son said, and from that, I knew he loved him. Why does *cancer of the throat* say love more than *throat cancer*?

"He's been asking about you. You know, he talks with a chalkboard. He writes it down. I'm assuming you're really busy, but he'd love to hear from you. It would be real important to him. And if you had the time to visit, I could pay for your ticket there."

"Where's 'there'?" I found myself asking.

"Oh, I thought you knew. Virginia Beach. My mom and him, they separated. She moved to North Carolina a couple years ago, but she's been back helping out since he's sick."

O-kay. So a better divorce than we had. But there were kids. My mom and Bruce Justin never had anything like that together. My brother and I were from a different father, whom we didn't know at all.

"What do you do?" I heard myself asking. So rude! My least favorite question at a Westside party! Harry, working on his pilot at my kitchen table in his boxers, did a double take. But I was so rawly curious! And the answer didn't disappoint. It was the kind of answer that the people who ask that question want but rarely get: it gave a clear view into class status, as crisp and stratified as a typed label in a museum. *Genus: Media materia masculum.*

The kid managed a concert hall in Ohio. Rock concerts, he said. I imagined yellowish work boots. No college or not much. Possibly smart in a carny way, like some key grips and production guys. That's how I pictured the rock-promotion world.

I kept asking around things. What I really wanted to find out was why this young man, twenty-eight years old, was doing everything he could to satisfy his dying dad's random whims. The answer was pretty obvious. He loved Bruce Justin. The man who had been a problem for me was, for this antler-wearing boy and his brothers, a good father.

* * *

These are the facts I knew about Bruce Justin: he was an orphan. The son of an English mother, he'd been raised in Buffalo, New York, and had no brothers or sisters, no family left whatsoever. My mother had not been in love with him. Like many women in the 1970s, she'd liked to model herself after Jacqueline Onassis, and, in our Wisconsin backwater, Bruce Justin bore some trace of resemblance to Ari. He had thick eyebrows and he held a position of prestige. He was second head coach of the Green Bay Packers.

They bought a ranch house. He tried with us. Our mother did too. For the only time in our childhoods, we had people over to our place for a holiday meal. The four years my mother remained married to Bruce Justin represented—on everyone's part—a goodwill effort to be a family in the way people did that, where we lived. We even had a succession of pets.

It didn't work, none of it did (the pets were left behind to sad, dubious ends), and I guess that should have been no surprise. Most halfhearted efforts don't work.

But there were weird things, too.

How weird, I was still not exactly sure.

They fussed over my body; they worried about how I wore my hair. I had put it in a ponytail; I remember Bruce Justin pulling out the rubberband and pushing my hair back to show my mother that my forehead was already too large. He was concerned that my hairline would recede. This was when I was twelve or thirteen.

"What am I supposed to do with it?" I said. Meaning my hair, which fell over my eyes.

They both felt strongly that I should have bangs. I refused. I'd never liked bangs. I still don't. Finally, I let it grow long and just hooked it behind my ears.

They also fretted over my hips. I remember Bruce's hands on my bones, as he told me to open my hips. Maybe this had something to do with posture? He said if I turned my hips out, it would help me jeté and turn à la seconde. I took ballet at that time, in a class where we were encouraged to wear belts over our leotards because it was thought that we had trouble distinguishing the locations of our waists. I was taking dance because I wanted to try out for the pep team.

"He was so proud of you! He watched *Marilyn's Sister* like twenty times," the son said, before we got off the phone.

Bruce Justin hadn't seen me since I was fourteen, a decade before I began to be myself. He belonged to a different life. I thought of sooted snow-drifts alongside a highway marked with car lots and fast-food chain restaurants. A dirtier life that I nonetheless remembered because I visited it at night, during sex.

I was lucky. The high school I'd been districted in, before we left, hadn't offered the requisite courses for admission to the state university. Thanks to that midnight getaway, I've had a profession. I'd gotten out of that polluted state and attended college in another part of the country. I'd married a handsome boy, from a softer life. Adam. My friends had been amazed.

"All these best-and-brightest guys," my brother said at the rehearsal dinner. "Nothing bad has ever happened to them. You wonder how they'll take it when it does."

We didn't have to wonder anymore. Now we knew. I was the something bad that happened to Adam Heller. I still thought of him as the Husband, after a decade divorced.

*   *   *

My aversion to sex started early in the marriage. To explain it, I said something. I said certain acts reminded me of my mother. Then he said the sentence I now think of as the one that ended our romance, though the marriage went on for years.

It wasn't only words. It was something I saw in his face. He was appalled by me. He felt cheated, as if he'd bought something spoiled. I didn't tell anyone about this for a long time. When I finally did talk to friends, I didn't repeat what he'd actually said.

But shouldn't the marriage have recovered? My husband wasn't the only innocently entitled young man resenting the trouble he'd found in a wife, once he got to know her. The next day, he bounded up the stairs of our apartment with a book. The author claimed that if you ever wondered whether or not you'd been sexually abused, you had been. It was ridiculous. But molestation was in the air those days. Anita Hill was on television, looking prim and beautiful. The older women who were our bosses snarked about her. *We've put up with worse*, they said. Or: *Every woman has to deal with that.*

Well, yes, but…, I thought but didn't say.

My friends and I had already whispered our various outraged confessions to each other. It had been a giddy relief to tell. Yet, as things went, in the sorrows and uses of women in the world, the trespasses upon us had not been so terrible.

Stepfathers had touched us. One friend had woken up with her stepbrother's tongue on her.

Steps, maybe they were the problem. Brought on by a generation of divorce.

*   *   *

That first time I talked to Bruce Justin's son, we left it that he'd check in and give me progress reports. As if I was one of the family. As if I cared!

Why did I agree to this?

The kid was sweet. But that wasn't all.

I was curious.

"How sick is he?" I asked, the next time the son, Kevin, called.

"Well. My mom's nursing him. The doctors say he won't make it more than a few weeks. He's asking to see you. I'm sure he'd like to talk to your brother, too. He wants you there for his death. He wants all his kids. He considers you his kids, too. I'd be real happy to pay for tickets. First class, you must be used to, right? I priced it out already."

Bizarrely, I said I'd go. I didn't know why. Still don't. I didn't have work. That's one reason. Like all actors out of work, I thought I might write a screenplay. And so I was looking for drama.

I said I'd buy my own ticket.

I called my brother. He declined, as I knew he would. Laughed and said, "Good on ya."

I flew coach.

On the plane I thought of my rom-com days in the city. (Rom-com cut with melodrama and farce: a cab ride paid for with quarters and dimes to a certain apartment in the East Village very late or actually very early, when the person who lived there might or might not answer his buzzer. The breathtaking suspense. That glory!) That had lasted about five years and fizzled out, a little before thirty.

I'd just begun talking to other young women then, really talking, in the way girls now do all through their childhoods. (I know from having a daughter.) It was a clear-eyed time. I remember it as a painting. Young Woman at a Bare Table, her chin propped on her arm, looking straight out of the canvas. Seeing Through No Gauze. Not one of my friends was frighteningly in love. We had been frighteningly in love already. That was over. We thought we were done with that forever; we understood what that had been, a kind of frantic anxiety, a terror, and we could do it this way now. We believed this way was better. Now we were beloved. We felt calm. We could work. This way was real. We were making deals for ourselves that a hundred years ago or right then, in another place on the planet, families were making for their daughters. We were becoming engaged to nice boys who were somewhat interchangeable. We compared them: their surprising talents for bread baking or neck massage, their gifts to us. We'd never compared the boyfriends who'd made us shudder.

"I love Adam, I'm just not sure *you're* feeling it," my brother once said.

"I *tried* feeling it," I said. "Remember? You were there."

My friends and I threw each other bridal showers. Strangely, this was the same time we started talking about sexual abuse.

Over a glass of pink wine one friend told us how she'd opened her eyes in the morning to her stepfather lying on top of her, his chin itchy and his breath foul, the way only the breath of someone much older can be. She was a person I very much admired. A designer of opera sets. Later, she art-directed two movies. Now she's a well-known decorator.

She'd taken a train to Washington, DC, to tell her divorced father what had happened. He was a congressman. He sat in his office, at a broad desk. "Was there penetration?" he asked his daughter, who was wearing a suit, black tights, and heels. She'd dressed up to tell him this.

"No," she said. There had not been.

After that, he changed the subject. He never brought it up again.

Our hostess refilled our glasses. She was the one who'd woken up in her own bed feeling her stepbrother's tongue inside her. When she'd jerked away, he'd said, "I just wanted to make you feel good." The rest of her years at home, she told us, she'd locked the bathroom door when she took showers and brought all her clothes in with her so she could come out fully dressed.

Everyone, it seemed, had been violated a little, though not one of us had been raped.

We were on our second or third glasses of pink wine, slicing strawberries when a silence fell. It was my turn to say something.

I remembered standing on the rim of the bathtub so I could see my whole body in the mirror and not liking what I saw. There were bulges I wished I could erase. I was more concerned with subtraction than addition, though some of that would have helped, too. Bruce Justin had commented that I could try to tighten my muscles and count to ten, five times a day. "Clench," he'd said, cupping the bulge at the top of my thigh.

I seemed to remember his hair wet, plastered down over his forehead like forked bangs. How was his hair normally? I really don't know. He was a stepfather my mother had left, so I'd probably have had to look hard to find him in the scattered pictures I'd once—as a family-hungry college girl—put together into an album. But as I remembered—or did I?—he stood in the shower with me, naked. He had his hand on his penis. "You can touch it," he said. "Go ahead and touch it. Don't be afraid of it. Touch it." Had this really happened?

All I could recall was his hair plastered down. His zipper smile.

I remembered nothing of his penis. If I'd touched it or not.

I never thought of him as good-looking or not good-looking. He was just Bruce. My mother and I made fun of him, when he wasn't there.

The blended-family thing hadn't really worked out so well.

*   *   *

That had been a bad time of my life; it wasn't only Bruce Justin. I was heavier than I'd ever been, before or since. One of the moms across the street told her wan daughter never to fight with me.

"That Julie is all muscle," she said. What girl wanted to be all muscle?

I'd take it now, I thought, looking out an oblong window at the plain Midwestern plowed land. I glanced over my fellow passengers. In front of me, two girls a little older than my daughter took selfies with their phones.

There had been a girl in my seventh-grade class, a large, powerful girl who wore a green parka and liked to lay sideways on a mattress we had in the basement to practice kissing. She said we had to practice for when the boys tried. I didn't want to but I did. And inside that warm green jacket, I knew I was being the girl. Her arms were huge and freckled; she wore her hair in a bowl cut, called that because Wisconsin women really did put a bowl on their children's heads and cut their hair around it, to make an even cap. I hated remembering her. I stopped myself and asked the stewardess for hot water with lime. I stopped myself thinking about the girl, even her name a bad taste, but I couldn't stop thinking altogether.

My mother. My mother was always hovering around a corner. I didn't really blame Bruce Justin. What broke me was my mother; she wanted to see me hurt. But could she have, really? One time they'd had men over, coaches from other cities. I was just out of the tub, getting ready for bed, my clean pajamas half-on.

"Go out. Just run in and let them see you," she'd said. "They've seen a naked girl before." I remembered her eyes shining, looking at my fat body. I didn't do it, little prude that I was. I buttoned my pajama top all the way to the top.

One of the coaches was a bachelor; he teased that he was waiting for me to grow up. But looking back now, it was pretty clear that he was gay.

The plane shuddered to a landing and we stepped out into verdant heat. It was moist. Gluey. The South in summer. I was glad to have tonight alone, a reprieve. The hotel in Richmond turned out to be fine, better than. I ordered room service. Read *Persuasion*. Every time I re-read Jane Austen I find I've completely forgotten the plot. I pushed away the thought that I was now too old to play anyone but Lady Russell. The marble bathroom was extremely clean, the sheets ironed or something. I don't know what hotels do to sheets to make them feel that way. I called the Husband.

It was Harry's bowling night. Harry bowled. Harry surfed. There were many issues. And Adam, after all these years, was still the one who understood my family, even though he'd never met my stepfather. No one had met my stepfather.

The Husband laughed with me on the phone. He still thought of Harry as the Hook-up. "How long are you staying?" he asked.

"How long do I have to?"

"Until the first flight out tomorrow morning. You could hop up to New York, get a car to the Hamptons. Or book a room in the city and shop. Come home Sunday. You have a child, Jule," he said, dropping his voice. "You don't have to do this."

An hour later the Husband called back. He'd located a car service in Virginia; he still found ways to pamper me. Even then, a decade divorced. The Husband had been pampered. He believed in it as a way of life—his whole family did, which is why I don't worry so much for our daughter, if something were to happen to me. We were still under his coverage, the way I continued to receive benefits from his Guild membership.

So shouldn't we have been able to find the path back, my lost husband and I? I wondered about this in the hotel. The worst of it hadn't been so bad. He would still tell me how a dress looked from behind, and at family dinners he could lift up a plate and remind me where we'd once bought the set on a ramble. We both remembered the blurry walks we took, carrying muffins and coffee, pushing the silver tricycle with our shining Nina.

But we'd never had real sex.

I'd found real sex with Harry. But Bruce Justin was there in the room, too. Oddly, it was the Husband with whom sex had felt wrong and incestuous.

I was the problem. In middle age, the mother of a twelve-year-old beauty, I could have sex and like it, but I couldn't be myself in it. I could be:

A fourteen-year-old with Bruce Justin, the age he was then, married to a stolid wife in a housedress—not my mother.

A male CEO picking up a slender girl, on a bus going to an Asian mountain temple.

Or a _____.

Or a _____.

The torrid list goes on. My own pornography already bored me.

Harry made me tell him everything. He pinched me sometimes in the middle of things, demanding, "Where are you? Who am I? Tell me."

He brought his portable computer and found girls. Most of them seemed to be nineteen or twenty, posing to look younger. He found some true amateurs, real kids. I wouldn't look at that. I made him shut the thing.

At first he had worried that I would go gay on him.

I tried to explain that I was no latent lesbian. "It's just how the dial was set for me, sexually," I said. "I'm working with what I have."

One night he wanted to bring a college girl over, to play in bed with us.

"No!" I screamed. "I never want that." This time I was the one appalled.

Harry suffered over that. He burst into my shrink appointment and accused the doctor of not dealing with my sexual issues. It reminded me of that long-ago time with the Husband, of the ridiculous book he'd brought home to help us—the author sounding an alarm: sexual abuse! The cause of all problems in the land! After Harry left, the poor shrink and I tried to talk about it. We finally agreed that there wasn't much there. And it wasn't that I didn't have *other* problems. Ask any actress in her forties.

There had only been two chairs in my therapist's office. Harry had knelt on the carpet by my side, holding my hand like an old-fashioned suitor.

He'd looked so concerned.

"It's only sex," I told him.

My older friends kept telling me that desire drains, at a certain age.

"That sounds awful," I said.

But they said, "Actually, it's not. Think of the unrestored Sistine Chapel. It's beautiful *because* it's muted. The *world* becomes more interesting."

When they put it that way, it sounded all right. Maybe I was ready to be over sex.

But I'd never have said that to Harry. Sex was what we had. We spent long afternoons in bed, talking about sex and through it and around it. After our first time, he'd sent me a list of ideas that involved pillows and positions for my hips. We'd get up from bed, make eggs and pasta, and then go back. He'd open his computer, find pictures of girls, and slowly we'd start again.

"I have to tell you something about me," I'd said to the young husband-to-be before I married him, but then I kept postponing it.

"You better tell me," he finally said, and worked himself up to a shrill frenzy. "I mean, you have to. If you killed someone or something… I'm not going to—"

We were on the couch.

"Come on, Julie, out with it," he said. "You have to."

I finally told him: I wasn't *really* blond.

In the morning, I canceled the Husband's car and driver. The Husband had always lived in cities. I liked driving through American wilds. In the rental Prius, I blasted HITS: Taylor Swift, Bruno Mars, Beyoncé. With the windows open, I drove barefoot.

Bruce Justin's son had already called. They were all waiting for me, he'd said.

Why? I didn't plan on staying long. I thought I'd arrive before noon, leave by three, drive back to the good hotel (I'd left my suitcase and booked a massage), and fly out the next day.

Though I'd never been here, the land outside looked familiar, not unlike Wisconsin. Weeds and untended fields all across central and eastern North America were similar enough to make you feel you were home.

He'd found me alone once, in the tiny front hallway of the ranch house where there was a coat closet none of us used. "Your mother's leaving me," he said. "And I want you to know I loved you and your brother."

Maybe he had. He had other uses for us, but maybe there was love, too.

He would be an old man now. I wondered what I'd find. I didn't really wish him well. But my mother had left him, maybe hurt him. We

were never sure why she'd done it. She'd said he was gay. A few of the
other coaches were, that seemed true. "He wanted to do funny things in
bed," she told me once. She'd said to my brother that she left because
she was afraid he would harm me.

But then he married a younger woman and had four boys.

What my brother and I always came to was that it had been a
mistake for her to marry him in the first place. So leaving him was just
a correction.

Once I'd been complaining, not about Bruce Justin, but about our
real father, whom we didn't know. I couldn't even go to tell him about
Bruce Justin, the way my friend had gone to her congressman-dad.
The woman I'd complained to, a studio stylist, said, "Yes, but he has
nothing. He doesn't know his children. Your mother is the one who
has everything."

She spoke calmly, a believer in Islam. She thought I had a fairy-tale
life; I'd seen evil, but was given good in the end. A rolling idea, like
the glass box of water she kept in her trailer; you could hold it in your
hands and tilt it to make waves. Sometimes I could see my life her way.

But I'd divorced, the worst failure you could have in civilian life.
I believed that. I thought maybe that's why the Husband and I were still
close: we were still trying to be forgiven by the other.

What he'd said that had ended our young love was, "I don't want
to have sex with my wife while she's thinking about her mother going
down on her!" He'd looked at me with horror. As if I was defective; he'd
married the wrong person and now he was stuck.

Could we have revived?

But we had already, in most ways. He booked me cars. We talked
together, calmly, with our daughter across a hundred restaurant tables.

The two friends of my youth were still with the men they'd married. The first years, the designer had beaten her young husband on his chest during sex. Now, though, her complaints concerned his long work hours and the way he only half-cleaned the kitchen.

It took me years to tell anyone what my young husband had said. I finally told Harry. "Does that make you see me differently?" I asked.

He shoved me onto the bed. "Kind of turns me on," he said.

Bruce Justin's house was better than I expected—bigger than the ranch house the four of us had lived in together. A *My Three Sons* house, split-level, with a two-car garage. I supposed coaches, especially coaches of winning teams, made decent money. (So much for the stylist's retributive justice.)

I parked in front. Because of acting, I'm usually aware of how I feel, entering a place, my level and degree of stage fright, the looseness of my hips. But I was surprised how cold my hands felt there on the sidewalk. Harry had helped me deal with terror, back when he was just my trainer, before we'd ever gone down, as he liked to say. He taught me to pick my soundtrack. When I had to walk into a room full of people where I sensed the threat of humiliation, he told me to memorize my song beforehand, run it for an hour three times a day until I could make it play in my head. Until I knew every chord, every word.

For now, here, today, I'd picked "Yellow." Coldplay. I heard it pounding.

The man who opened the door had blond facial hair. Not quite a beard, but more than a day's growth, not the way men wore it in New York or LA.

"I'm Kevin," he said. "The one you talked to."

"Good to finally meet you," I said, and it kind of was. We shook hands. He looked older than twenty-eight.

Kevin's brothers were grown men with flannel shirts tucked into jeans and substantial guts. I didn't remember Bruce Justin having a belly. Their mother, Betsy, wore a white blouse embroidered with pansies, her hair what we used to call permed, a color between brown and gray. They gave elaborate and embarrassing attention to my old jacket and invited me to sit in the still, unused living room.

"How was your drive?" one of them asked.

I murmured something short. This was excruciating. I didn't want a session of small talk with strangers.

"I can bring you in," the mother finally said. "He'll be so glad you're here. We told him already that you were on your way."

I stood up, and the sons stood up, too. What did I expect from Bruce Justin? I wondered, following his estranged wife. A confrontation? A naming of ancient crimes? But what would that get me? What could even an apology possibly mean, all these years later? And if he did apologize, was I supposed to forgive him?

In the middle of a suburban home, a sickroom. Across from the hospital bed, a TV flickered, showing my first feature, *Marilyn's Sister*. I played Marilyn Monroe's sister, Berniece Baker Miracle, and I suppose in it, I looked the closest to how I was when he knew me. Still no bangs, I thought, glancing at the girl on the seventeen-inch screen. In the old footage, I was beautiful—why couldn't I have seen that then, or at least appreciated that that was as good as it would ever get?

Bruce Justin was emaciated, his hair awful, shaved on the sides.

When he smiled his smile, looking at me, it was the same zipper smile. Evil.

His wife held her hands together at the front of her jeans. One of the brothers had a camera. They wanted to snap pictures of all of us standing around Bruce Justin's bed. This took awhile, because the one with the camera had to trade places with another one, so there could be a picture with him too. I offered to photograph them—the wife and sons and Bruce Justin. They were the family. But they demurred. The wife came back with a tray of Cokes in glasses with straws.

It was strange to see him old. I'd used him, in the dark, but I'd always seen him the way he was years ago, when I knew him. My mother, whom I'd visited all along for the requisite holidays, was the one who had changed, who had grown into her age. I hardly ever thought of her the way she'd been then.

After a while of no one saying anything, Kevin, whom I'd already decided I liked the best, asked if I wanted to be alone with his father.

"Yes," I said, surprising myself, then immediately regretting it. Would he try to touch me? He couldn't really move now, it didn't seem. But he could look at me. All of a sudden, I remembered a phrase from when I was young: girls would say, *He got it off of me.* Sex was a kind of theft, then. Afterward, you had less; he had more.

But nothing happened when Bruce Justin's family filed out of the room. He looked at me with weak eyes. What did I want to be alone with him for? I finally understood the word *dumbstruck.*

What, exactly, had he done? Was it what I remembered or more? Were the memories just chips of something that, if I were a diligent excavator, I would have put together by now? I recalled good things, too. My brother and I in the back seat as he drove to The Forum, the restaurant near the sports arena, where everyone met up after the big games, for prime rib and baked potatoes. Bruce Justin and my mother talking in the front seat like partners, like parents.

All this resolved to a little fluttery wave of my hand at him. "Hey," I whispered, sitting in a chair near the window.

Bruce Justin made sounds. He pointed to the small chalkboard that sat on his bedside table. I jumped up to hand it to him.

I follow your career, he scratched with the chalk. *You did well. Proud.* He pointed to a stack of DVDs—my filmography. *The Third Boleyn*, *Zombie Christmas*, even a *Simpsons* episode I'd done a voice on.

He smiled and his smile went from evil to something else, something made-up. What did he want with me? I'd thought it was possible he would apologize.

But that was mostly all he had to write. His eyes closed for a moment. I could see he was tired. He seemed like a stranger. Whether the man I could picture, his expression like the stab of a steak with a fork, had harmed me or not, seemed to have nothing to do with this person now.

I sat there for more of the day, the brothers and Betsy coming in and out occasionally, treating me like some British royal, every time offering me a *beverage*, that word, and food. The house was extremely clean, but it smelled faintly chemical, like a hospital, not a home. One of the sons was a cop, his wife a teacher. Another a salesman of water-ski equipment. The youngest managed a Petco.

I was aware of being richer. I felt thin.

I wanted to get out.

I just didn't want to eat anything there.

As the light began to wane in the small windows, I stood up to go. I had to ask for my jacket.

"You're not going to stay for dinner?" Betsy said. I saw their dining table, faux Regency, elaborately set with cloth napkins and chargers under the plates (chargers!) for ten or twelve people.

"We thought you'd want to eat before that long drive. And I have the bed made up in the guest room."

They all looked at me. I knew they wanted me there. Kevin mumbled, "My girlfriend, Serena, the one who wrote to your agent, she's coming too."

But I just couldn't take it.

I wondered, though, if before I left I should say anything true, even to Kevin, or to his mother. Then she said, "He's helped so many people in the area." They told me he ran a sports arena here, and directed a program for underprivileged boys.

"He was always the pro," Kevin said, shaking his head.

I went into the room one more time and told Bruce Justin I was leaving. He opened an arm to hug me. I bent down, braced for the touch—as minimal as I could get away with, I thought. But a wave of revulsion hit. I can't even say what sense it was—smell, feel. It wasn't sight; I'd closed my eyes. That was as close to knowing as I'll ever get.

He wanted to write one more thing on his chalkboard. You could see his agitation. It took him some time. *Your mother*, he wrote down. Then he made little circles with his hand by his forehead: the universal sign for cuckoo. He shrugged his shoulder and smiled as if he was laughing, then shook his head.

"He thought she was crazy," Betsy said, apologizing for him.

I slipped into hating him again and left.

At the time, it all felt like nothing much. A wasted weekend. A mistake. I drove fast back to the hotel, not noticing any evening smells of local flora or fauna. I had the concierge book the last plane out, paid for the unused room, skipped my massage and got the hell out of Dodge. Somewhere over Nevada I realized, with a jolt, that he hadn't even asked about my brother. If I was supposed to forgive him, it had been a total bust.

In the next year, though, my life changed. I took the lead on a cable show Harry wrote. Playing Chrissy, a schizophrenic high-school principal who has to keep everyone around her from knowing about her condition, is the most demanding role I've ever had. I'm still growing in the part, in season three, two Emmys later. The writers and I are giving each other the best work years of our lives. Ratings are good, as are overseas sales. We play prime time in England, which is incredible, with no British stars. The studio sees the arc stretching seven seasons.

Kevin called me when Bruce Justin died. It was during up-fronts; I was in New York, but I didn't go down for the funeral. I sent expensive flowers. Since then we've kept in touch. His girlfriend, Serena, wanted to be an animator, and when she first came out to LA we gave her a tour on the set and called around to PDs we knew. She got a job at Fox on the staff of the *My Favorite Martian* remake, moved out, and lived with three other kids in North Hollywood. Kevin tried for a long time to find work in the music industry and couldn't, but finally took a job managing the old Troubador on Sunset, where I once saw Donovan Leitch sing. Nina, my daughter, loves Kevin and Serena. When they last came over for dinner, Serena braided a green feather into Nina's hair.

For the after-party of last year's Emmys, I changed from my beaded gown into something easy. I'd had jeans and a shirt delivered to the restaurant, one privilege of being older and the lead. When I was leaving, someone made a joke about Harry being the same age as Serena. She said, "I'm not here with him, I'm with her." The person who made the joke whistled. "We could do it, Jules," she said. She winked at me. I saw the men's torsos sink and swivel, their breath taken. I tossed her my balled-up gown. It was an expensive gown by an Arab Parisian designer, but I was leaving with Harry, carrying home an Emmy. I thought that at her age I would have loved someone to throw me a dress. And someone did. Many someones. Serena just happened to catch mine.

I had what I needed, not from Bruce Justin, but maybe a little from him, too. Those nights riding in the backseat to The Forum. Anyway, I got out. And now that he's dead, I don't mind Kevin and Serena. I actually like them. They're family, steps of a kind, I suppose.

The Husband and I never got back together, as I contemplated for a dwindling second in that Virginia hotel, but we still talk on the phone about Nina six times every day. Harry has moved in. We figured out a trick—I start with whatever fantasy comes to mind, he makes me tell him, he plays along, he's unfortunately a terrible actor and that's distracting sometimes, but when I get close, when I'm almost there and it's too late to stop, he pinches me and makes me look at him, into his face. Then we fall together. No more Bruce Justin. I have that feeling of when it begins again after a heartbreak, as if the world is opening up shop, the sun is lifting, something has already started and you're in it. It's a beginning. Another beginning.

MONA SIMPSON *is the author of six novels, most recently* Casebook.